DANCE DIVAS

Showstopper

DANCE DIVAS

DANCE DIVAS

Showstopper

Sheryl Berk

BLOOMSBURY
NEW YORK   LONDON   NEW DELHI   SYDNEY

First published in the United States of America in April 2015
by Bloomsbury Children's Books
www.bloomsbury.com

Bloomsbury is a registered trademark of Bloomsbury Publishing Plc

For information about permission to reproduce selections from this book, write to
Permissions, Bloomsbury Children's Books, 1385 Broadway, New York, New York 10018
Bloomsbury books may be purchased for business or promotional use. For information on
bulk purchases please contact Macmillan Corporate and Premium Sales Department at
specialmarkets@macmillan.com

Library of Congress Cataloging-in-Publication Data
Berk, Sheryl.
Showstopper / by Sheryl Berk.
pages   cm   — (Dance Divas)
Summary: Anya is just getting used to being the newest member of the Dance Divas when
her parents want her to move back home to L.A. to study dance "more seriously," which
means she may have to say good-bye to Divas forever. The timing couldn't be worse.
City Feet is back with a vengeance at the Smooth Moves Competition in Las Vegas.
ISBN 978-1-61963-576-0 (paperback) • ISBN 978-1-61963-575-3 (hardcover)
ISBN 978-1-61963-577-7 (e-book)
[1. Dance teams—Fiction. 2. Dance—Fiction. 3. Friendship—Fiction.] I. Title.
II. Title: Show stopper.
PZ7.B45236Sg 2015   [Fic]—dc23   2014034288

Book design by Donna Mark
Typeset by Newgen Knowledge Works (P) Ltd., Chennai, India
Printed and bound in the U.S.A. by Thomson-Shore Inc., Dexter, Michigan
2 4 6 8 10 9 7 5 3 1 (paperback)
2 4 6 8 10 9 7 5 3 1 (hardcover)

All papers used by Bloomsbury Publishing, Inc., are natural, recyclable products
made from wood grown in well-managed forests. The manufacturing processes
conform to the environmental regulations of the country of origin.

To Pam Kaplan,
K-kids forever XO

Table of Contents

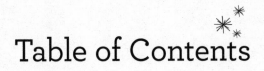

DANCE DIVAS

Showstopper

CHAPTER 1

Give Me a Break

Toni Moore rarely allowed her Dance Divas elite team a week off from rehearsal. There were simply too many routines to learn, too many costumes to fit, not to mention an endless list of competitions from coast-to-coast. But this time, as she contemplated the calendar tacked on the bulletin board outside studio 1, Toni drew a huge red "X" across Presidents' Week in February.

"No way! No dance for a whole week?" Rochelle asked her teacher as she passed her in the hallway. "Is the world coming to an end?"

Toni sighed. Rochelle knew just how to push her buttons. "I simply decided to give us all—especially myself—a much-needed break since school will be closed here in New Jersey." She raised an eyebrow. "Unless of course you'd prefer to be in the studio those days practicing your pointe technique?"

Rochelle shook her head. "Nope. I'm good with it!"

She rushed off to the dressing room to share the news with the rest of her teammates.

"Really? A whole week off?" Scarlett cheered. "That's amazing! Maybe I can convince Mom to take us to Florida for some sun and fun."

"Yeah, Disney World!" her little sister, Gracie, piped up.

Bria checked the calendar on her phone. "Great. I can get in some extra studying for my algebra test, start my science fair project, and write my English paper on *A Midsummer Night's Dream*."

"Seriously? You're free from Toni and all you want to do is study?" Rochelle asked her.

"I don't *want* to study. I *have* to study," Bria said, correcting her.

"Not everyone can be as naturally brilliant as you are, Rock," Scarlett teased her.

"Or as naturally beautiful," Rochelle replied, laughing.

"I think I'll tag along with my mom to Hollywood." Liberty suddenly jumped into the conversation. She was polishing her nails a perfect shade of Ballet Slipper Pink. "She's choreographing a new music video."

"Is it for someone famous?" Bria asked. Liberty's mom, Jane Montgomery, was one of the biggest choreographers in the music biz.

Liberty grinned. "Isn't it always?"

Rochelle rolled her eyes. "Here comes the name-dropping," she whispered to Scarlett.

"Beyoncé was just saying how much she adored my mom's last video for Ariana Grande . . . ," Liberty bragged. "But I think the one Mom did for Britney was far more creative."

"So she's choreographing Beyoncé? Or Ariana? Or Britney?" Gracie said, jumping up and down. "Can I go, too?"

Liberty patted the little girl on the head. "No, Gracie, dear. It's only for professionals."

"So how come your mom lets you go?" Gracie protested. "You're not a professional."

Liberty frowned. "Because I act like a professional, that's why."

"And because she nags her mom day and night till she finally agrees to take her if she'll just stop whining," Rochelle said.

"I can whine," Gracie said. "Scoot says I'm really good at it. If I do, will you take me?"

Scarlett nodded. "She's right. She's a professional whiner."

"See?" Gracie pleaded with Liberty. "Pretty please?"

Rochelle chuckled. "Aw, come on, Liberty, give the kid a break. Call up Beyoncé and tell her you're bringing a friend. Oh, wait—you don't actually have Beyoncé's number, do you?"

"At least I have somewhere exciting to go," Liberty insisted, pointing a finger in Rochelle's face. "What are you going to do with your week off? Sit and watch the grass grow? Change your baby brother's diapers? It's not like your family has a lot of extra money to go on a vacation."

Rochelle stood up. "You take that back."

Scarlett jumped in between them—as she always did—to referee. As the unofficial team captain it was her job to keep the peace and remind them of what Miss Toni would expect. Toni ran a tight ship, and wouldn't stand for anyone rocking the boat.

"Guys," Scarlett said, "do you recall what Miss Toni threatened to do to anyone on her team who isn't getting along?"

"She said they won't be allowed to go to Smooth Moves in Las Vegas," Gracie piped up.

Both Rochelle and Liberty backed down—there was no way either of them was going to miss out on a trip to Vegas—or one of the biggest dance competitions in the country. And they knew Toni meant business when she made a threat.

Anya strolled into the dressing room with her dance bag slung over her shoulder. "What did I miss?" she said, noticing Rochelle and Liberty glaring at each other.

"Oh, just the usual," Scarlett said.

Anya turned to Liberty. "Did you insult Rock again?"

"She started it," Liberty said grumpily. "But I'm willing to forgive and forget. I'm the bigger person."

"You're certainly the bigger mouth," Rochelle muttered under her breath.

Bria tried to change the subject—anything to keep those two from fighting. "Anya, did you hear the news? Miss Toni gave us Presidents' Week off! The whole week!"

Anya's eyes lit up. "Really? I've been dying to go home to L.A. and see my family."

"You miss them a lot, don't you?" Scarlett asked her.

"I do. Especially my big brother, Alexei. He's the coolest." She found a photo on her phone of a tall teenage boy with blond hair and blue eyes at the beach and showed them.

Rochelle grabbed the phone out of her hands. "Wow. You never told us you have a cute brother!"

"And *you* have a boyfriend," Bria reminded her. "What would Hayden think of you drooling over Anya's brother?"

"I wasn't drooling," Rochelle said, wiping her mouth with the back of her hand. "I was just looking."

"Alexei's an amazing surfer—he taught me how to ride waves just like him," Anya told them. "He's going to be a really famous filmmaker one day—he's always shooting movies. He even has one of those cameras you wear on your head. He wore it last week skating down the pier in Santa Monica. He got the most amazing video of people's feet!"

"He sounds weird," Liberty interjected. "Who films feet?"

"He's just really creative, and he's always there for me," Anya explained. "When my parents didn't want me to come join Divas full-time here on the East Coast, he convinced them that my mom and I should move here. He's my biggest fan."

Scarlett smiled. "Then you should text him and let him know you'll be home soon," she said. "Get the surfboards ready."

CHAPTER 2

The Luck of the Draw

When they reported to the studio for technique class, the girls could hardly contain their excitement.

"Why do I hear chattering?" Toni asked. She had her back to the class and was studying her binder filled with dance notations and schedules. "This is a *silent* warm-up."

The girls obeyed but Anya couldn't help beaming as she stretched at the *barre*.

"Very nice, Anya," Toni said, looking up and noticing her *cambre back*. "Your flexibility has improved a lot these past few months."

Toni took a seat on her stool at the front of the studio. "I suppose you've all heard the news by now. I've decided to close the studio over Presidents' Week for vacation."

Gracie's hand shot up. "Liberty's taking me to meet Beyoncé in Hollywood!"

Liberty groaned. "I never said that."

"I'm sure you all are excited to make plans," Toni continued. "I would just like to remind you that two weeks later, we are competing at Smooth Moves. City Feet will be there as well, and losing is not an option."

"Can't Justine give it a rest?" Rochelle complained. City Feet's coach—and Toni's archnemesis from her ballet school days—was always trying to outdo the Divas.

"No, she can't," Toni replied. "And I guarantee her team isn't resting either. I'm sure they're working straight through the holiday week. Which means we have to work ten times as hard now if you want to have those days off."

Toni then dug into her tote bag and pulled out a deck of playing cards. "See these?" she asked her team. "I want each of you to pick one."

"Is this a magic trick?" Gracie asked. "Are you going to make a card appear behind my ear?"

Toni tried not to laugh. Gracie was the youngest member of the Divas, with the most active imagination. "No, Gracie. It's my idea for our group choreography and costumes." She held the deck fanned out in front of her. "Pick."

Gracie pulled a card out and looked at it. "It's a 'joker,'" she told the group.

"Well, that's appropriate," Liberty said, smirking. She was the next to choose and drew the queen of hearts. "And so is my card! I'm the queen!"

Each of the girls pulled their cards as well: Rochelle was the jack of spades; Scarlett was the king of clubs; Bria was the ten of diamonds; and Anya was the ace of hearts.

"The card you chose will inspire your costume," Toni instructed them. "I don't want a giant playing card made out of cardboard for this routine. I want something that's flashy and fabulous and worthy of Las Vegas."

"I'll have my mom call Lady Gaga's costume team," Liberty volunteered.

Toni shook her head. "Nope. No costume designers, no moms, just you. I want you to make your own costumes so you are truly invested in this number."

Liberty looked shocked. "I don't sew!" she protested. "I don't even own a needle and thread. My mom has people who do that!"

Rochelle elbowed Scarlett. "Oh, this is gonna be good."

"Couldn't I get a teensy-weensy bit of help?" Liberty pleaded with her teacher. "I hear Katy Perry's designer isn't very busy at the moment . . ."

But Toni put her foot down—literally. She stamped her heel on the studio floor. "Enough! I want to see a sketch of your ideas and some fabric swatches by this weekend."

When they got back to the dressing room, Bria immediately tore a sheet of paper out of her notebook and started sketching.

"I think I should do a black leotard and skirt covered in shimmering faux diamonds, don't you?" she asked Anya.

"Don't ask me," Anya insisted. "The last time you BeDazzled our costumes for our duet, it was a fashion disaster."

"It wasn't that bad," Bria replied.

"Really? It was so heavy I could hardly move! And the stars kept flying off and attacking the judges!"

Bria shrugged. "Well, this is different. I'll make sure the diamonds are superglued to the dress and don't fly off."

"What does a joker wear?" Gracie asked.

"He's kind of a clown," Anya explained. "With a silly hat and pointy shoes."

Gracie studied her card. "I could do pom-poms on the hat and collar."

"And two different colored tights for your legs," Scarlett suggested. "Something really fun. I'll help you, Gracie."

Gracie shook her head. "Uh-uh. I'm doing it all by myself. Miss Toni said so."

"My ace of hearts is going to wear a red tutu," Anya said, envisioning her design. "Maybe with a white satin bodice—and red lace fingerless gloves?"

"Do you think I should wear a mustache?" Rochelle asked, looking at the dapper gent on her playing card.

Scarlett also noticed the jack had curls in his long blond hair. "You definitely gotta do that 'do," she said, giggling.

"Yeah, well, your king has curls in his beard!" Rochelle pointed out.

"But I get to wear a cool crown," Scarlett replied.

She suddenly noticed Liberty was very quiet. "Your queen has a crown, too," she told her. "That should make you happy, Liberty."

Her teammate just sat, staring at the card in her hand, not saying a word.

"I think she's still in shock that Miss Toni nixed having someone do her work for her," Rochelle whispered to Scarlett.

"It's not so bad, Liberty," Anya tried to reassure her. "I mean, you have great taste in fashion. Maybe this could be the start of something big! Your own dancewear line!"

Liberty got up from the bench, gathered her dance bag, and stormed out of the dressing room.

"Was it something I said?" Anya asked.

"No, she's just upset," Scarlett said.

"Or planning something sneaky and underhanded," Rochelle added. "Do you *really* think Liberty Montgomery is going to make her own costume?"

"But Miss Toni said no helpers," Gracie insisted. "Those are the rules."

"And since when does Liberty *ever* follow anyone's rules but her own?" Rochelle said. "You just wait and see. She'll find a way to wiggle her way out of it."

CHAPTER 3

Designing Divas

When Saturday rolled around, Toni ended acro class fifteen minutes early and asked each of the girls to show her their costume design ideas.

"I like the tutu," Toni said, examining Anya's sketch. "Let's do matching red pointe shoes with it, and a headpiece with tulle and hearts."

Anya took notes carefully. "I was thinking maybe some red sequin hearts on the white bodice as well. Or is that too much?"

Toni nodded her approval. "This is Vegas. More is more. It's the one time you girls can go a bit over-the-top with your costumes and the judges will eat it up."

That was good news for Bria, who had already stocked up on yards and yards of rhinestone-beaded fringe to sew on her black velvet leotard. "I was thinking these could make a skirt of diamonds," she explained to Toni.

"My only concern is that all the fringe will tangle and might get in the way of your dancing," Toni said. "But I love the fascinator hat and long black gloves. See how it feels when you try it on, but I do think it's very Vegas." She looked around the studio. "Who's next?"

Gracie emptied a large plastic bag at her feet. Scraps of different fabrics, buttons, trim, and assorted pom-poms spilled out. "I was thinking I could stick them here and here," Gracie explained, holding pom-poms up to her head and shoulder.

Toni looked lost. "I don't understand," she replied. "Is your costume polka-dotted, or are the pom-poms just trim?"

Gracie considered. "Okay, I could do that."

"No, Gracie. I don't want to tell you what to do. I want you to make some design decisions. Why don't you give it some more thought."

Gracie gathered up her costume bits and baubles and shuffled to the back of the room. Scarlett was up next.

"So my king wears a crown—around his waist," she said, showing Toni a sketch of a gold skirt with a jagged hemline that fanned out to look like a crown. "I could BeDazzle it with different colored jewels."

"And what about the top?" Toni asked.

"I was thinking maybe a red, long-sleeved leotard topped with a faux fur–trimmed white vest," Scarlett replied, pointing to the king's outfit on the playing card. "He looks very luxe."

Toni nodded. "I'd like to see some kind of a headpiece as well. No royal would leave his or her head crownless."

"Then you'll love my idea!" Liberty suddenly spoke up. She unrolled a large sheet of paper from a cardboard tube. "Ta-da!"

On it was a photo of Queen Elizabeth of England dressed in her finest royal robes. On her head was a huge platinum, diamond, pearl, ruby, and sapphire crown with a puff of purple velvet beneath the open frame. "Behold! The Imperial State Crown!" Liberty said, waving the poster in Toni's face. "It's made of platinum with a 317-carat diamond on the front and the Black Prince's Ruby in the center. It contains more than 3,000 gems, and Queen Elizabeth wore it after her coronation."

Toni stared. "And do you intend to call Her Majesty up and borrow it for Smooth Moves?" she asked.

Liberty chuckled. "Of course not! I'm going to make my own version—the Imperial Liberty Crown!"

Toni rubbed her temples. "I think it's a stunning crown, but not doable."

"Well, of course it's doable," Liberty insisted. "And since the crown I'm making will be so spectacular, I'm going to wear something simple to go with it."

"Simple? Does Liberty ever wear anything *simple?*" Rochelle whispered to her teammates.

"Okay," Toni said, nodding her approval. "If you can pull it off, go for it. It'll certainly catch the judges' eyes."

"Not fair!" Rochelle whispered to Scarlett. "Liberty always gets her way!"

Toni heard her—or just guessed that she would be complaining about Liberty's royal headgear. "If you're so eager to speak out of turn, Rochelle, why don't you come up here and present your design?"

"Rock it, Rock!" Scarlett said, giving her friend a pat on the back.

"Well, my design doesn't have diamonds or jewels or even pom-poms," Rochelle began saying.

She handed her teacher a drawing she'd made of a black spandex catsuit topped with a vest covered in red, black, and gold zigzag stripes. "I know it's nothing fancy. I thought maybe I could sew a black velvet spade on a red baseball cap and maybe wear it backward. The hat this guy has on doesn't really work for me. It kinda looks like a pineapple upside-down cake."

She showed Toni her playing card and the jack's flat-topped gold cap adorned with red circles.

"I like it," Toni replied.

"Really? I gotta wear a cake on my head?"

"No, I like *your* design," Toni said. "It's colorful and contemporary, and it will be easy to move in. Good job."

Rochelle waved at Liberty, who was fuming.

Toni picked up her clipboard and checked off "Costume Design" on it. "Aside from Gracie—whom I would like to stay after class today—you can all start sewing." The girls picked up their bags and sketches and ran out of the studio.

"Remember," Toni called after them, "when we get back after the break, it will be full steam ahead on our dance numbers. Get some rest—you'll need it."

CHAPTER 4

Joking Around

Gracie hung back and waited for Miss Toni to stop digging around in the closet and call her over. She was sure her teacher was going to scold her for not doing her design homework like the rest of her teammates. But the truth was, she had lots of ideas for her joker costume—and that was precisely the problem! She couldn't whittle her design down to just one or two things that worked well together—she wanted to use them all. She was great at making costumes for her dolls at home, but when it came to her own outfit, especially one that was supposed to be both funny *and* fabulous, she had a hard time figuring out where to start and what to edit out.

"Ah! Here it is!" she heard Miss Toni say as she pulled a red garment bag off the rack and laid it down on the floor in front of her. "This is what I was looking for."

She unzipped the bag to reveal a patchwork dress made of dozens of scraps of different colored and printed fabrics. "This was for a dance I choreographed called 'Crazy Quilt,'" Toni told her. "See how no two pieces of fabric are the same?"

"Uh-huh," Gracie replied. "It's pazy."

Toni smiled. She was slowly learning to pick up on Gracie's lingo. "Definitely pazy—pretty and crazy at the same time. That's what your joker costume should be. Let's have a look at that bag of stuff you brought in."

Toni also brought out a plain white leotard and leggings. "What if you stitch all these scraps on like this," she said, placing them this way and that on the legs. "See? No rhyme or reason to it. No pattern. Just whatever tickles your fancy."

"But it's not a fancy costume," Gracie insisted. "Not like Scoot's or Bria's. And I'm not sure I'll be able to dance in something that tickles."

"'Whatever tickles your fancy' means whatever you like," Toni explained.

"Oh!" Gracie replied. She began to piece the scraps together till they formed a colorful collage. "Can I use the pom-poms, too? Maybe on the bottom of the pants so they jiggle when I dance? I think that would be fun."

Toni nodded. "So do I. Why not add them around the neckline and the wrist cuffs as well? And leave the hat and shoes to me."

"Really?" Gracie asked. "But you said no helping, and that's helping."

"It can be our little secret," Toni said with a wink. "Besides, I said no helping from moms or Lady Gaga's costume team. I never said no helping from your teacher."

Gracie pretended to lock her mouth and throw away the key. "I won't say anything—not even to Scoot," she promised.

"Good," Toni said, handing Gracie the leotard and leggings. "I wouldn't want to ruin my reputation as a tough teacher."

Gracie shrugged. "I'm not sure what that means, but I don't think you're a tough teacher. I think you're a nice teacher." She hugged Toni around the waist and dashed out of the studio with her fabric, pom-poms, and a plan in hand. She ran into Anya and dropped all of her materials on the floor.

"What's the rush, Gracie?" Anya asked, helping her clean up the collision.

"I've just gotta get to work on my costume," Gracie explained. "I have so much to do!"

"Oh, so it's a fashion emergency?" Anya teased her. "Need some help?"

For a moment, Gracie considered. It *was* a ton of scraps to stitch on to the leotard and leggings, and threading a needle could be a little tricky. Still, she had made a promise to Miss Toni.

"I can't. No help."

Anya smiled. "Okay. I understand. You want to sew solo."

"Exactly!" Gracie said, crawling on the floor to salvage a few more buttons that had fallen from her bag.

"Well, what if I just spot you?"

"Like if I was doing a back tuck off the balance beam in gymnastics?" Gracie asked.

"Just like that," Anya said. "So if you're cutting some fabric or pinning something down, I've got your back. No helping, just spotting."

To Gracie the gymnast, it sounded perfectly reasonable.

"K-dokey," the little girl replied. "You can be my official costume spotter."

They worked together for over an hour—Gracie stitching, Anya threading and cutting—until Scarlett came out of her stretch class to collect her sister.

"Wow, that looks amazing, Gracie," she said, admiring the patchwork design. They'd gotten most of the legs and part of the arms covered in fabric squares.

"Anya didn't help—she was just spotting me," Gracie insisted.

"I knew that," Scarlett said, smiling. "This costume has Gracie written all over it."

Gracie held it up to the light. "It does? Where?"

Scarlett chuckled. "I mean, it's got your style and flair."

"Oh," Gracie said. "Yeah, it's jokeriffic, don't ya think? The pom-poms were all my idea."

Anya pretended to bow to Gracie. "I just watched Gracie work her magic."

"Funny you should say that," Rochelle said, strolling out of studio 2. "Miss Toni just told me that you and I are doing a magic duet at Smooth Moves."

"Do you think you'll pull a bunny out of a hat?" Gracie asked Anya.

"Or make Liberty disappear?" Rochelle joked.

Anya wouldn't even hazard a guess. Who knew what trick Miss Toni had up her sleeve this time! She'd just have to wait till after the break to find out.

CHAPTER 5

Santa and Sushi

The minute Anya told her mom about the week off, she jumped on her computer and booked two plane tickets to Los Angeles.

"Your father is going to be so happy," she told Anya. "He was just complaining that he wouldn't get to see us until spring break in April."

To Anya, it felt like forever since she'd seen her brother and dad. Technically, it was two whole months—they had both flown in to see her perform in *A New Jersey Nutcracker* in December. Anya had hoped they would stay for Christmas and New Year's, but Alexei had midterms to study for, and her dad had an endless amount of dental emergencies to tend to.

"You wouldn't believe how many people chip a tooth on holiday fruitcake," he said, kissing her on the forehead. "An oral surgeon's job is never done." He could see the disappointment in Anya's eyes. "I'm sorry, honey, but we can't stay more than a week."

That was the only part she didn't like about being a Dance Diva—living 3,000 miles away from her home. The small apartment she shared with her mom in Scotch Plains, New Jersey, was barely big enough for a tabletop Christmas tree. She knew her father would be decking the trees in their front yard with colored lights and blowing up the giant seven-foot-tall inflatable Frosty the Snowman.

"Aren't you too old for that stuff?" her mom had asked when she griped that their apartment had no chimney for Santa to make his grand entrance on Christmas Eve.

"There's no age limit on Christmas," Anya said. "I love Frosty and leaving Santa cookies and milk."

Her mom held up a box of vanilla ladyfingers. "Think Santa would be okay with these?" she asked. "Or I could make some tiramisu if you're trying to impress him."

Anya knew her mom hadn't been much in the holiday spirit those days and not even a visit from Santa could fix that. Every time her dad called, she went on and on about how cold it was and how many feet of snow was on the ground. Rochelle and her family had invited them over for Christmas Eve dinner, and they said yes, but it just wasn't the same.

"My mom makes the most awesome sweet potato casserole with mini marshmallows on top," Rochelle had announced, passing Anya the dish around the dining room table.

Mrs. Hayes blushed. "I'm sure Anya and her mom make a lovely Christmas dinner, too."

"We do! We have sushi," Anya piped up. "And borscht—that's cold beet soup."

Rochelle pretended to gag. "Eww. Raw fish and beets for Christmas?"

"I'm from Malibu and my husband is from Moscow," Mrs. Bazarov tried to explain. "We combine our cultures. The kids love it."

Anya nodded. "I love eel and California rolls."

"Well, I hope you won't be too disappointed," Rochelle's dad added. "I'm afraid all we have is honey-glazed ham, no eel."

"That's okay," Anya said, helping herself to a slice. "This is yummy, too."

"Save room for dessert," Rochelle reminded her. "Apple pie and ice cream."

Rochelle's baby brother, Dylan, clapped his hands together in his high chair. "Icy cweam!" he squealed.

"After you finish your peas, Dylie," Mrs. Hayes said, spooning a few in his mouth. "Veggies first, then ice cream."

When the table was cleared, Anya carried in a platter of Russian tea cookies she and her mom had baked from scratch.

"It's my babushka's secret recipe," she said, waving the powdery, white doughy circles under

Rochelle's nose. "They melt in your mouth. And I love how they look like snowballs."

Rochelle sampled one and her eyes lit up. "Amazing!" she said, licking the sugar off her fingers. "Babushka can bake!" She popped another—and another—in her mouth. "What's a babushka?"

Anya laughed. "My grandma from Russia," she said. "I know it's a silly name."

Rochelle shook her head. "Not that silly. We call my grandpa Pappy Hee-Haw," she volunteered.

"Not to his face," Mr. Hayes said, chuckling. "His name is Herman."

Rochelle was fascinated. "What other Russian words do you know, Anya?"

Anya thought for a moment. While her dad was fluent, she only knew a handful of Russian expressions.

"I don't suppose you know how to say 'let's eat'?" Mr. Hayes asked, trying to wrestle the plate of cookies away from Rochelle. "Rock is hogging them!"

"I think your Christmas sounds cool," Rochelle said. "Eel and all."

"It is," Mrs. Bazarov said with a sigh. "Which is why we miss it so much. It's the first Christmas we're not together as a family."

"But you're with us." Mr. Hayes raised his glass, trying to brighten the mood at the table. "And we're lucky to have you. Cheers!"

Anya raised her water glass and clinked it with Rochelle's. "Thanks for inviting us, Rock," she said. "If I can't be in L.A., there's no place else I'd rather be."

CHAPTER 6

Home Sweet Home

C U Soon Anya texted Alexei. As she packed her suitcase, she daydreamed about hitting the waves with her big brother.

Her brother read her mind. **Surfrider Beach first?** he replied.

"You almost forgot your pointe shoes," her mom said, coming into her bedroom and tossing them on top of her pile of clothes.

"Why? I thought this was supposed to be a dance-free vacation?" Anya asked.

"Just in case you want to go pay Miss Natalya a visit," her mom replied.

Until Toni, Anya had never met a dance teacher as tough as Miss Natalya. She made Anya practice for hours at the *barre*, until every muscle ached and she was drenched in sweat. She remembered how demanding her ballet teacher was, but also how she pushed her to be a better dancer.

"Your *frappé*—it is no good!" Miss Natalya would scold her. "It needs to be like a match, striking the floor, yes?"

Anya had tried to picture how she would swipe a match to light it: the action was fast, firm, direct, explosive. She did the same with her foot, flexing it then extending it out in front of her. This time, her *frappé* was quick and strong.

"Da! Da! Yes! Yes!" Miss Natalya cheered.

All Anya ever wanted to hear was those words, so she worked her hardest to please her. When Anya decided to give up ballet for competitive dance, Miss Natalya had been very disappointed.

"We spend all these years together and then you leave your studio for what? Some team?"

"It's not just a team. It's a competitive dance team," Anya had tried to explain. But she didn't expect her ballet teacher to understand how excited she was to showcase her talent somewhere beyond the *barre*. "They go all over the country! Last week they were in Baltimore."

Miss Natalya hung her head. "And Baltimore is exciting to you? When you could be a prima ballerina one day? You throw that away?"

Anya was determined. "I am not throwing my ballet away. I'm just expanding my horizons."

Her teacher turned her back and walked away, muttering some words in Russian that Anya couldn't make out.

"I'm sorry, Miss Natalya," she called after her, "but this is what I want to do."

During her first few months with the Shooting Starz team in L.A., she had won a handful of

Teen Solo trophies. Then Justine spotted her at a competition and asked her to join City Feet in Long Island.

"It's really a no-brainer," the dance coach had told Anya and her parents. "My team wins. All the time. Do you want to dance with the winners or the losers?"

It meant quickly relocating to the East Coast and getting a tutor. But from the moment she met the rest of the City Feet girls—Addison, Phoebe, Mandy, and Regan—she understood *why* they racked up so many first-place trophies. They were *that* good and *that* determined.

"I can't even do a cartwheel," she complained, watching Mandy, the team's "Tiny Terror" execute a flawless acro combination without even breaking a sweat.

"Well, you better learn," Justine insisted. "Everyone on my team is expected to toe the line."

"She means either keep up or drop out," Addison translated. "No excuses."

So Anya worked day in, day out, learning to master City Feet's trademark moves. In only six weeks, she was performing explosive hip-hop routines, whirling *fouettés*, and flawless back handsprings. She even picked up a perfect chin stand.

"You're catching on," Miss Justine complimented her. But she also knew that Anya was their secret weapon when it came to the Solo division.

"I'm going to have you do a classical ballet routine *en pointe*," she told her. "Should be a breeze for you, right?"

What she didn't tell Anya was that she was entering her in a category that was below her age. When the judges found out that she was thirteen and not twelve, Anya was disqualified, points were deducted from City Feet's score, and Justine was issued a warning for "unsportsmanlike behavior." It was embarrassing but also a wake-up call: Anya realized that City Feet would stop at nothing to win.

"This isn't what we signed up for," Mrs. Bazarov told Justine. "We don't teach our daughter to be dishonest."

Justine shrugged. "It was a misunderstanding. These things happen."

But her mother stood her ground. "Maybe, but not to us. We're going back to L.A."

That's where she was when Toni first flew out to meet with her. Her parents had called Toni shortly after the City Feet fiasco and begged her to put Anya on her team.

"Please let me join the Divas," Anya pleaded when she met with Toni. "All I want to do is help you beat City Feet."

"Really? Because if that's all you want to do, then my answer is no," she said.

"What? I thought you hated Justine?"

"Hate is a strong word," Toni insisted. "Let's just say I want to win just as badly as Justine does—but I won't sink to her level. Is that clear?"

Anya nodded. "I don't want to lie or cheat either."

"What *do* you want to do?" Toni asked.

Anya thought for a moment. "I want to dance. I love it more than anything, and I want to be the best dancer I can be."

"Good," Toni said, extending her hand to shake. "Then we have a deal. Welcome to the Divas."

It had taken several weeks to convince Scarlett, Liberty, Rochelle, Bria, and Gracie that she wasn't just a spy for the opposing team. But eventually, she won them over. Now, none of them could imagine the team without her—and she couldn't imagine being without them.

Anya looked miles away in thought, so her mother waved a hand in front of her eyes. "Did you hear a word I just said?" she asked.

"Uh-uh," Anya answered. "I was thinking."

"Well, I was thinking, too. I was thinking you owe it to Miss Natalya to stop in. Your father says she can't wait to see you again."

Anya raised an eyebrow. "What do you mean? How would Dad know that?"

Her mother continued folding clothes into her suitcase. "Oh, he just ran into her at Vons supermarket."

She tried to picture Miss Natalya pushing a shopping cart down the frozen-food aisle. She didn't think her teacher had any life outside of the ballet studio.

"Seriously?" Anya asked. "What did she say?"

"Oh, nothing," her mom said. "Just that it would be nice to see you in class again."

Anya rolled her eyes. "Well, I don't take classes with her anymore. I'm a Diva now, remember?"

Her mom nodded. "You may be a Diva but you don't have to act like one. There's no harm in visiting your old ballet studio."

Anya had a sinking feeling that there was more to the story than her mother was telling her. But she was too excited to be going home to argue with her. "Fine. I'll stop in and say hi. But these . . ." She took the pointe shoes out of her bag. "Stay here."

CHAPTER 7

I Love L.A.

The flight from Newark to LAX seemed a lot longer than usual, probably because Anya was so anxious to touch down. While her mom napped, she made a mental list of everything she wanted to do as soon as they got home: go shopping on Melrose with her best friend, Poppy; grab a hot dog at Pink's; take a long walk on the beach barefoot.

"Please fasten your seat belts and prepare for landing," the pilot's voice boomed over the loudspeaker.

"We're here! We're here!" she said, shaking her mom awake.

Her mother opened one eye. "Already? That was quick. I could have used a few more hours of shut-eye."

She had to practically drag her mother by the arm through the airport into baggage claim. "Mom, hurry up!" she pleaded with her.

"Anya, honey, we have a whole week here. What's the rush?"

"I have so much to do," Anya insisted. "I want to get it all in."

When they exited the airport, Alexei and Anya's dad were waiting at the curb in their convertible. Mr. Bazarov kissed his wife before sweeping Anya up into a huge bear hug.

"Wait! Wait! I gotta get this on film," Alexei shouted, grabbing his camcorder out of the glove compartment. "Okay: lights, camera, action!"

Anya stuck her tongue out toward the lens. "Did you get that?" she asked, laughing. "Do you ever give the moviemaking thing a rest?"

Alexei shook his head. "Do you think Hitchcock ever stopped rolling? Or Spielberg?"

"You're Bazarov—not Spielberg," Anya told him.

"But you could definitely play E.T.," he teased her. "You've got that big-alien-head thing going."

Anya suddenly noticed he was getting behind the wheel. "Wait! Did you get your license?"

"I did!" her brother replied proudly. "I am officially a California State–licensed driver."

"Awesome!" Anya squealed. "Can you teach me?"

"Whoa!" her dad interrupted. "One teenage Bazarov on the freeway is plenty. You see all these new gray hairs?"

"You should see me on the I-10," Alexei bragged.

"No, trust me," her father said. "You want to keep your eyes closed. It's better that way."

Her mom laughed. "Well, what are we waiting for? Let's go home!"

As they pulled into the driveway, Anya noticed that everything looked exactly the same as she had left it. The mailbox was still painted bright blue with BAZAROV on it in yellow letters. The front yard still had a white picket fence around it, and her mother's begonia bushes were in bloom.

"Wait till you see your room," Alexei teased her. "I gave it an extreme home makeover."

"No, you didn't!" Anya shrieked. "Mom!"

"He's kidding," her father reassured her. "But I did give the kitchen a fresh coat of paint."

"Without asking me?" her mom shouted. "No, you didn't!"

"Kidding!" Anya's dad and brother sang in unison.

Anya pushed open the front door and bolted up the stairs to her bedroom. She held her breath as she turned the knob and opened the door. There was her pink canopy bed; her giant stuffed giraffe, Percy; and her autographed framed poster of prima ballerina Misty Copeland on the wall.

"See? Told ya I didn't touch it," Alexei said, peeking in. "Your smelly ballet shoes are still under the bed."

Anya lifted the comforter and peered underneath the bedframe. There—just where she had put them—were more than a dozen pair of beaten-up ballet slippers.

"My collection," she sighed. "Thank goodness!" Each pair had a very special significance in Anya's ballet career: they marked every first and last day of each level she'd been in. They were a symbol of her progress from primary to Level 6, and she loved to stand them next to each other and compare how much her feet had grown over the years.

Anya flopped down in her white, fuzzy beanbag chair and kicked off her sneakers. "This feels so good," she said, closing her eyes. "I missed this."

"I didn't miss your snoring through the wall at night," Alexei teased.

"I don't snore!" Anya insisted, tossing a throw pillow at her brother's head.

"Do to," he said. "You sound like Dad's lawn mower."

"Well, you'll only have to suffer for a week," she said.

"I wish it was more," Alexei said, sitting on the edge of the bed. "It's lonely around here with no one to pick on."

"You could always drive Dad crazy," Anya pointed out.

Alexei shook his head. "Not the same. He doesn't take the bait like you do." He looked around the room and his eyes settled on the wall behind Anya's head. Suddenly, his face went pale. "Look out!" he shouted. "There's a giant tarantula climbing up the wall!"

"EEEK! Where?" Anya shrieked. She jumped out of her chair and grabbed her tennis racquet out of the closet. She sliced through the air, swinging it wildly. "I got it! I got it!"

Alexei fell on the floor, laughing. "Oh, you got it all right!" he said, cracking up. "I got you!" He zoomed in on her face with his camera.

Anya dropped the racquet to her side. "Seriously? There's no spider?"

"Like I said," her brother smirked. "No one takes the bait like you, Anya."

It was almost reassuring to know that her brother could still pull her leg after all these months apart.

"Fine. You got me," she admitted. "I'm still terrified of spiders."

"Aww, you mean this little guy?" Alexei asked, pulling a tiny black insect out of his shorts pocket.

"EEEK! Get it away from me! Get it away!" Anya screamed jumping up on the bed.

"Relax! It's a rubber spider!" Alexei laughed. "Awesome scream, though, for my movie." He checked the replay. "If this footage doesn't get me into film school, I don't know what will."

"Are you still planning on going to college to study film?" Anya asked.

Alexei nodded. "Absolutely. I've applied early decision to my top two: UCLA and Tisch at NYU. Fingers crossed. I could hear any day now."

"NYU?" Anya gasped. "You're thinking of going to college in New York City? That's super close to Mom and me! That would be awesome!"

"It's my top choice," Alexei added. "Do you know that Woody Allen went there?"

"And you're going to make your little sis the star of your first big movie, right?" Anya reminded him.

He dangled a rubber spider in her face. "We'll see!"

Downstairs, Anya's parents were busy catching up—and discussing how they were going to break the big news to their daughter.

"She's going to be so disappointed," Mrs. Bazarov said.

"Felice, we talked about this. We have to do what's best for us as a family."

Anya burst into the living room and flopped down on the couch next to her dad. "Alex is crazier than ever!" she said. "His practical jokes are out of control!"

"Tell me about it," her father said, putting his arm around her. "You don't have to deal with him every day."

"But wouldn't it be nice if we did?" her mom suddenly interjected.

"No!" Anya said. "One spider psych-out is enough for me."

"I mean, wouldn't it be nice to be back living here in L.A.? All together as a family?" her mother continued.

"It would—if Dance Divas was here," Anya said. "But it's not."

Her parents shot each other a concerned look.

"So I think you and Alexei should hit the beach, then meet us for sushi at Wok 'n' Roll for dinner," her dad said. "Sound like a plan?"

"Sounds like a great plan," Anya replied. "As long as you check his pockets first for rubber spiders."

CHAPTER 8

A Change of Pace

While Anya was in L.A., Liberty was in Holly-wood, Scarlett and Gracie were in Orlando, and Bria was busy hitting the books, Rochelle was bored silly.

"You can't just lie around all day staring at your phone," her mom said, prying the iPhone out of her hand. "Find something to do."

"I was doing something!" Rochelle replied. "I was texting Scarlett. She's on the Dumbo ride. I never thought waiting in line for two hours to get on a flying elephant would sound appealing, but it does."

"If you're bored, then why don't you clean out your closet?" her mom suggested. "Or entertain your brother? Or crack open a textbook?"

Rochelle pretended to yawn. "Boring, boringer, boringest."

"Then how's this for a plan," she said, handing her daughter her dance bag off the coatrack in the hall. "Head down to Divas and get in some extra practice."

Rochelle mulled it over. Busting some moves while the studio was empty over the break didn't sound all that bad.

"Fine, I'll go practice," Rochelle agreed.

"Thank you!" Her mom heaved a sigh of relief. "I was afraid your butt was going to become glued to that sofa!"

Rochelle had never seen the studio so deserted. All the rooms were empty and dark, though she could hear loud, pulsing music coming from somewhere. She followed the noise down the hallway to Toni's office and pressed her ear against the door. She listened intently, straining to make out the song. It had a heavy beat and a cool rhythm but it also sounded a bit classical.

Suddenly, the door opened and Rochelle fell inside the office.

"May I help you?" Toni asked, clearly annoyed.

"Um, no, I was just . . ."

"Spying? Eavesdropping? Poking your nose where it doesn't belong?" Toni fired back.

She noticed her teacher was dressed in a pair of billowy pants and a crop top. Her hair was long and pulled back into a loose ponytail. Rochelle tried not to stare, but it was hard not to. Toni looked *strange* for Toni. She never came to class in anything but a leotard, ballet skirt, and bun.

"Are you doing hip-hop?" she asked her teacher.

"If you must know, it's a form of dance that I've never personally performed, and I'm trying to perfect my moves."

Rochelle shook her head. "But that's just the thing. Hip-hop isn't ballet or jazz or even acro. There is no 'perfecting' it. It's spontaneous and loose. It's just gotta come from the music."

"Well," Toni huffed. "Since you think you're such an expert, perhaps you'd like to come work with me in the studio and you can give me a hand."

"Me? You want *me* to teach *you* hip-hop?" Rochelle gasped.

Toni handed her the boom box. "I'm still the teacher," she reminded Rochelle. "Let's not forget that, shall we? I'm working with a new form of hip-hop—like a fusion of ballet and street—and I need to try it out on someone."

Rock followed Miss Toni into studio 2, where they both quickly pushed the *barres* to the back of the room. She pointed to a spot for them to take their starting position.

"You don't want to be too stiff," Toni said, showing her. "Feet should be hip-width apart. But I want the arms and legs to be less lock and pop, more ballet. Get it?" She demonstrated a kick ball change while gracefully pumping her arms to the sides.

"You could also do this," Rochelle suggested, *pirouetting* in her sneakers while crossing her arms in front of her chest. She rolled her shoulders and slid her feet across the floor in a series of lightning-quick steps.

"Exactly!" Toni said, "I saw Charles 'Lil Buck' Riley jookin' and I was inspired."

Rochelle's mouth fell open. "You follow Lil Buck?" she asked. "He's amazing! He does pointe in sneakers!"

"It's Urban Ballet," Toni corrected her. "And I love it. It's very forward-thinking, very this generation."

"It's very cool!" Rochelle said enthusiastically.

"So you're up for working it into your duet with Anya?" her teacher asked. "If we could fuse both of your styles, ballet and hip-hop, into one, I think your dance would take first place."

Rock smiled. "You had me at hip-hop, but first place works, too."

Meanwhile, Bria found a way to study and stay limber at the same time. She sat on the floor with her legs in a straddle and her English book on the floor in front of her.

"That does not look very comfortable," her mom said, watching her stretch.

"It's not supposed to be comfy," Bria insisted. "It's supposed to be good for my middle split."

"Ah," Mrs. Chang replied. "How's your term paper coming along?"

Bria sighed. "It's not. It takes me forever to read just one page of A Midsummer Night's Dream. None of it makes any sense!" She held the book up. "Just look at this! Who talks like that?"

Her mom took the book and read aloud: "'Awake the pert and nimble spirit of mirth!'"

"See what I mean?" Bria said, groaning. "It's gibberish."

"Theseus is just saying he wants to throw a party," her mom explained.

Bria sighed. "I just don't get it."

Her mom nodded. "I think I have something that might help." She held up a pair of tickets to the New York City Ballet. "They're performing *A Midsummer Night's Dream* tomorrow night. I thought maybe we could go together. Seeing it might help you better understand the story."

Bria's face lit up. "You mean get out of the house and go see a ballet? Do something besides study?" She pulled herself out of her straddle and jumped to her feet. "I'm in!"

Mrs. Chang smiled. "When I was younger, I felt the same way about Shakespeare. Until my father took me to see *Hamlet* at a local theater."

"Did you like it?" Bria asked.

"I thought it was the most magical thing I had ever experienced," she recalled. "The lines were spoken but they had a musical quality to them."

Bria remembered that her mom studied violin for many years. "So thinking about Shakespeare like a song helped you get it?"

"Exactly!" her mom replied. "And I hope seeing *A Midsummer Night's Dream* as a dance will help you get it as well. Sometimes, it's stressful tackling something new. So you need to see it in terms you can relate to."

Bria considered what her mom was saying. "That makes sense . . . I guess." Her mom flipped through the book and found another line. "I think this one describes you," she said with a smile.

Bria picked up the book and read Helena's quote: "'Though she be but little, she is fierce!'"

Bria giggled. "I love it! Maybe that should be the Divas' new motto! I guess Shakespeare knew what he was talking about after all!"

CHAPTER 9

Back to Ballet

While Bria and Rochelle were trying to find something entertaining in their time off, Anya was just looking forward to being lazy. She refused to set her alarm clock, and was annoyed when her mother knocked on her bedroom door bright and early.

"Rise and shine, sleepyhead," she called. "We have a fun day ahead!"

Anya opened one eye. "It's vacation. Don't I get to sleep late?"

Her mother opened the door. "Not if you want to go see your old ballet friends at Dance Academy West."

Anya groaned. "Mom, they have to be at 9:00 a.m. pointe class. I don't."

"Well, I thought maybe you'd want to pop in before class. You know, chat with everyone in the dressing room? Say hi to Miss Natalya?"

When her mom got something in her head, she was like a dog with a chew toy. "Fine," Anya said, sighing. "You're not going to leave me alone until I go, are you?"

"Nope," her mom replied. "I made your favorite blueberry pancakes for breakfast. So up and at 'em!"

The studio was thirty minutes away in downtown L.A. "Look! Nothing's changed!" her mom said as they pulled up to the gray brick building.

"It never changes," Anya said. "I stuck my chewing gum under the bench out front when I was five years old and I bet it's still there."

"But you had some great memories here," her mom tried to convince her. "All those recitals, spring shows, that adorable butterfly costume . . ."

"It was a moth," Anya pointed out. "A gray moth that flittered around Poppy, who was a flame, remember? And the costume was really itchy."

"It was your first recital and you were precious," her mom insisted. "You go say hi and I'll wait here in the parking lot for you."

As she walked through the door of Dance Academy West, Anya recognized a few familiar faces.

"Anya! You're back!" a tall blond girl said, racing toward her.

"Well, just visiting, Amanda," she replied, giving the girl a hug. "Do you know where Poppy is?"

Amanda pointed down the hallway. "She's in a private right now with Miss Natalya. Go peek!"

Anya strolled down the carpeted hallway, stepping over the dancers sprawled on the floor stretching. She stopped to look into the studio windows. Each group wore different colored leotards: there were the tiny pink level 1s; the red level 2s; the green level 3s; and the purple level 4s. Level 5 and up wore black—which is what Poppy had on along with a pair of well-worn toe shoes. Anya looked inside the window of studio 4 and saw her old ballet teacher twisting her bestie's leg into a pretzel. She couldn't make out what she was saying to her, but she was sure it was the usual: "Nyet! Nyet! No! No!"

When Miss Natalya noticed her visitor at the window, she motioned for her to come inside. Anya turned the knob and the door creaked as she pushed it open.

"Ah, look who we have here!" Miss Natalya said, holding out her arms. "She returns!"

She pulled Anya into a hug so tight Anya could barely breathe.

"Hi," Anya replied. Her teacher still smelled of strong perfume and even stronger coffee.

"Me next!" Poppy said, running to her friend. "Anya-bananya!"

"Poppyseed!" Anya said, laughing.

Miss Natalya smiled. "It's like you never left, yes? Did you bring your leotard and shoes?"

"No," Anya said, staring down at her feet. "I'm taking a break this week."

"A break? Dancers never break!" her teacher shot back. "You eat, sleep, and breathe dance." It sounded like something Miss Toni would say!

"As you can tell, nothing has changed around here," Poppy whispered.

"But you've changed!" Anya insisted. "You got your braces off!"

Poppy smiled to show off her straight teeth. "I got them off last March. Wow, how long has it been since we saw each other?"

"Too long," Miss Natalya replied. "I'm glad you changed your mind."

Anya looked puzzled. "Changed my mind? About what?"

"About coming back to the studio," Poppy said. "Maybe we can duet for the spring showing!"

"Wait, what? I'm not coming back to the studio," she told her friend. "I have a huge dance competition in Las Vegas in a few weeks."

Now it was Poppy's turn to be confused. "But your mom told my mom you were moving back to L.A. I was so psyched! Aren't you excited, too?"

Anya felt her cheeks burn. She was furious! How could her parents have said such a thing? And was it true? Were they really thinking of making her quit Divas and move back home? She had to get to the bottom of this . . . now.

"I gotta go," she apologized to her friend as she rushed out of the studio. "Text you later."

CHAPTER 10

Diva No More

Anya was seeing red. She didn't even shut the car door behind her before she started yelling.

"How could you?" she asked her mom. "How could you and Dad just make a decision and not even ask me?"

"Honey, calm down. It's not like that."

"It isn't? Poppy said you told her mom we were moving back to L.A."

"Your father and I think it would be for the best."

Anya gasped. So it was true. "The best? This is the worst news I've ever heard!"

Her mother sighed. "We tried to make it work, but it's too difficult being on two different coasts. We're a family. A family should be together."

Anya buried her head in her hands. She, Rochelle, Scarlett, Liberty, Bria, Gracie, and Miss Toni were a family, too. And she felt like she was being torn away from them without any warning. What was she going to tell the Divas? What could she say?

Her mom read her mind. "I'll explain it to Miss Toni. I'm sure she'll understand."

"But *I* don't understand," Anya insisted. "Can I at least go to Vegas with the team in March?"

"I'll do my best to convince your dad," her mom promised. "Can you try and look on the bright side? You'll be back at ballet with Poppy."

"I'm not the same girl who went to DAW," Anya insisted. "I can't just come back and forget about all my new friends and everything I've learned."

"No one is asking you to forget," her mom assured her. "Divas will always be a special part of your life."

Anya wished she had earplugs so she could tune out everything her mother was saying. Maybe if she closed her eyes, she'd wake up from this nightmare, and none of it would be happening.

When they reached their house, Anya opened the door and bounded up the steps. She slammed her bedroom door behind her and dialed Rochelle's number.

"Hey, how's L.A.?" her friend answered. "Seen any good movie stars lately?"

"My parents are making me quit Divas," Anya sobbed.

"What? Why? When?"

"I guess they're tired of living on opposite coasts," she replied.

"You can't leave! Not now!" Rochelle protested. "It's just not fair."

"Tell me about it," Anya replied. "I don't get it. Why let me join Divas and move to New Jersey in the first place if they were just going to take it away from me?"

"I know it stinks, but maybe they thought it would work," Rochelle suddenly considered. "Maybe they really hoped it would."

"So that's it? I just turn in my Divas jacket and go back to studying ballet with Miss Natalya? Or join another team and compete against you?" Anya exclaimed. "Doesn't anyone care what I want?"

"You don't have to turn in your jacket," Rochelle replied. "Once a Diva, always a Diva. You know that."

Anya dried her eyes with her sleeve. "What do you think Miss Toni will say?"

"Not much." Rochelle tried to picture her teacher's face, learning that one of her best dancers was quitting. "I think she'll just be worried about how we can win without you."

"Smooth Moves will be my last competition as a Diva," Anya said. "*If* my dad says I can do it. I don't know how I can dance knowing that."

"You'll do your best. You always do," her friend assured her.

After her call, Anya went downstairs to talk to her parents. They were seated at the kitchen table, waiting for her to calm down.

Her mom poured her a glass of lemonade. "Did you call Rock?" she asked. "Did she make you feel any better?"

"The only thing that would make me feel better is if you said you changed your mind," Anya said, perching on a stool. "I don't suppose you have?"

"There are tons of dance schools here in L.A.," her father insisted. "I know, I know—not Dance Divas. But plenty that are just as good. If you don't want to go to DAW anymore, that's fine. We want you to be happy."

"Then let me stay with my team and my friends!" Anya pleaded. "That's the only thing that will make me happy!"

"We're in L.A. and you and your mother are in New Jersey. It's not a good situation for any of us," her father said, raising his voice. "We hoped you would be able to see and understand that."

Just then, Alexei came in the door carrying his camera and a tripod. "Whoa," he said, sensing the tension in the air. "Maybe I should come back later?"

"No!" Anya said, grabbing her brother's arm and dragging him into the kitchen. "Stay. You get a vote, too."

"A vote? What am I voting for?" Alexei said, helping himself to a soda in the fridge.

"Whether or not I stay in Dance Divas in New Jersey or move back here."

Alexei popped the lid on his can and took a long sip. "In my humble opinion," he began, "I think Anya has done really well with her dance team. If you've got a good thing going, I say stick with it."

"You see?" Anya cheered. She could always count on her big brother to take her side. "That's two for, and two against."

"Regardless, our minds are made up," her father said sternly. "I'm sorry, Anya. The best I will do is let you compete at Smooth Moves. But that's it. That's your last competition as a Diva."

CHAPTER 11
Keeping Secrets

The week in L.A. flew by, and before she knew it, Anya was back at the Divas Studio Monday afternoon. Gracie was running up and down the halls in her Mickey Mouse ears from Disney World, and Liberty was showing off the selfies she'd taken on the set of Pitbull's new video.

"Did you have a fun vacation?" Scarlett asked Anya.

Anya tried to smile and sound convincing. "Yeah, it was great." But she was dreading having to break the news to her dance coach. She could just picture Miss Toni's face: stern and hard as a rock. She hoped she wouldn't explode and start screaming at her. Everyone wanted to be on the Dance Divas Elite Competition Team. There was a line a mile long of girls just waiting for a spot to open up. And here she was, quitting! How could Toni *not* be furious and insulted?

"I guess I should get to rehearsal," Anya said, taking a deep breath and steeling her nerves.

Rochelle had promised with a double-pinky swear that she wouldn't say a word to anyone until Anya broke the news to their teacher. "You want me to come with you and talk to her before class?" Rochelle asked her.

Anya shook her head. "No, thanks. I want to wait till the time is right."

As the girls began stretching at the *barre*, Miss Toni took her seat at the front of the studio and began studying her notes. Anya knew better than to interrupt her when she was concentrating. Maybe *after* class was a better idea?

"Welcome back, ladies," Toni said. "I hope you haven't picked up any sloppy habits on your week off." She looked at Rochelle. "Like sickled feet."

Rochelle quickly corrected the position of her foot and continued with her *tendus*.

"I'm going to go over our plans for Smooth Moves," Toni continued, glancing at her clipboard. "Scarlett, I'm giving you a solo," she said.

Scarlett's face lit up. "Thanks! What is it?"

"It's a modern routine called 'Superstition,'" Toni replied. "You'll dance barefoot."

"Modern?" Scarlett whispered. "I'm not that great at modern."

"Not being great has never stopped you before," Liberty said, smirking. "Why should it stop you now?"

Toni mulled over the duet with Rochelle and Anya. "This is a very complicated Broadway routine with real magic tricks in it," she said, facing Anya. "But I think you're ready for it. Anya, how do you feel about pairing with Rochelle for 'Magic to Do'?"

"Um," Anya hesitated. "Miss Toni, I think I need to tell you something . . ."

Rochelle elbowed her. "Not now!" she whispered. "This is an awesome duet and we get to do it together."

Toni raised an eyebrow. "Yes, Anya. What is it?"

"I, um," Anya said, twirling a strand of her ponytail nervously. "I really like your lipstick. It's so pretty. What do you call that color?"

Toni looked surprised. "My lipstick? It's red," she said. "And if we're done chatting about cosmetics, can we get back to the specifics of our group dance number?"

Anya nodded. "Sure. Thanks."

Toni rolled out a platform consisting of three steps on all sides and placed it in the center of the studio floor.

"Think of a deck of cards being shuffled," she instructed her pupils. "Gracie, you are front and center at the top. Rochelle, you stand in front of her; Bria behind her, and Liberty and Scarlett on either side. Anya, the ace starts offstage in the wings." She pointed to the right side of the studio.

The girls took their formation. "Now duck down like this," she said, tucking Rochelle's head into her chest. "Gracie, you do a straddle jump over her shoulders like you're playing leapfrog."

Gracie obeyed and landed a few feet in front of Rock on the floor. "The rest of you, stretch your arms up and to the sides. Then touch the ground and come up into a handstand."

Anya waited patiently as Toni perfected each girl's balance and posture. Then Toni motioned for her. "Anya, *chaînés*," she commanded. Anya spun gracefully until she reached the center of the studio.

Toni chewed on her pencil eraser. "Not bad. Not bad. The spacing is off, but I think it'll work. The question is, is it strong enough to win?" She went back to scribbling notes on her clipboard.

"My mom heard that Justine is hiring some big-time guest choreographer from Hollywood for the Smooth Moves competition," Liberty reported. "The guy's unbeatable."

"When you say unbeatable . . . ," Bria asked.

"I mean he has *never* choreographed a dance that did not take home first place," Liberty replied. "Ever."

Rochelle groaned. "Thanks for the news flash, Liberty. That makes us all feel great."

"I'm just saying what I heard," Liberty defended herself. "I could be wrong—but then again, I'm *never* wrong."

Miss Toni didn't like the sound of that. "We'll just have to beat the unbeatable then," she said.

"How do we do that?" Gracie asked.

Toni crossed her arms over her chest and looked determined. "With no distractions. Each and every one of us must be focused and at the top of her game. Is that clear?" All heads nodded. "I'll be right back," she said, "I think I'm going to need to break out the trampoline . . ."

When their teacher was out of the studio, Rochelle breathed a sigh of relief. "Phew! It's a good thing you didn't tell her, Anya. Toni is really focused on taking Justine down. You heard what she said: no distractions. You can't tell her now."

"Tell her what?" Gracie interjected.

"Nothing," Anya insisted. "It's a secret."

Gracie's eyes got big. "A secret? What kind of a secret?"

"Uh-oh. Now you did it," Rochelle said. "Never say the word 'secret' around Gracie."

"Hey! I'm a good secret keeper!" Gracie protested. "Aren't I, Scoot?"

Scarlett shrugged. "It depends. If the secret is something *you* want to keep—like when you hid my favorite pair of leg warmers—then yes, you're really good at it."

"See?" Gracie said. "I didn't even tell you that Miss Toni is helping me with my costume. Oops!"

"I can't tell you my secret, Gracie," Anya replied. "Not now."

Scarlett looked worried. "Are you okay, Anya? Something isn't wrong, is it?"

Anya didn't know what to say. She hated lying to her friends.

Gracie pouted. "Well, when can you tell us?"

Anya looked to Rochelle for help. "I don't know."

"She can tell us all after Smooth Moves is over," Rochelle suggested. She squeezed Anya's hand. "Right now, we have some Feet to beat."

CHAPTER 12

Viva Las Vegas

The Luxe Hotel was one of the fanciest and flashiest on the Vegas strip—and where Liberty's mother, Jane, had insisted her daughter and the rest of the Divas stay during the Smooth Moves competition.

"It's fabulous! Didn't I tell you?" Liberty asked as they climbed out of their taxis from the airport to check in. "Mom always stays here when she's choreographing one of Britney's shows."

"It's really bright," Bria said, shielding her eyes from the flashing multicolored lights surrounding the lobby entrance. "And ginormous."

"It's obnoxious if you ask me," Rochelle said.

"Well, no one did," Liberty tossed back. "It was very nice of Mommy to make sure we all had suites with king-size beds and Jacuzzis. Did I tell you that Selena Gomez stayed in my room last weekend?"

Toni held up her hand before the argument could escalate. "It was very kind of Jane to arrange for our hotel stay," she said. "And I'm sure the rooms are lovely. But we're not going to be spending any time in them today. We need to get to the convention center to rehearse."

Liberty made a "boo-hoo" face. "Aww! I was really looking forward to lying around the pool and soaking in the hot tub. Mommy arranged for a private cabana and everything!"

"The pool can wait," Toni insisted. "Unless you all feel like losing tomorrow."

Rochelle shook her head. "Not a chance. Whatever City Feet is bringing, we can top it."

Toni sighed and handed her luggage to the bellhop. "Let's hope so. You never know what tricks Justine has up her sleeve."

It was tough dragging the girls out of their posh suites, but they all knew there was little time to waste. When they got to the Las Vegas Convention Center, it was already packed with dance teams pouring in from all over the country.

"Stay here," Toni instructed them. "I'm going to pick up our paperwork and badges. And remember: no talking to the competition." She tapped Gracie on the head. "That means you. We wouldn't want to give anything away."

Gracie frowned. "Why does everyone think I can't keep a secret?"

"Because you can't," Scarlett reminded her. "You have loose lips. Remember when we got Mom those new headphones for her birthday and you spilled the beans a week early?"

"You didn't say it was a secret," Gracie insisted. "You just said 'Keep it under wraps.' So I wrapped the headphones and gave them to her."

Rochelle chuckled. "That's classic!"

Bria hushed them all. "Don't look now, but we're being scoped out. They look pretty fierce." She motioned to a group of boys wearing tuxedo jackets with their team name RAZZMATAZZ written on the back in gold sequins.

"As if!" Liberty replied. "They have no taste in fashion, so they can't possibly be a threat to us."

"What about them?" Anya pointed to a group of six girls in pink hoodies that read PINK LADIES ROCK.

"Boring!" Liberty said, yawning. "Honestly, I don't see one dance team here that stands a chance of touching us."

But she spoke too soon. Suddenly, the City Feet team was standing right behind them.

"Oh, look! It's the Dance Duds!" Regan said, laughing. "Ooh, I'm scared! NOT!"

"Wow, does someone smell LOSER in the air?" Addison asked.

Rochelle gritted her teeth. "And look who we have here! Justine and her four dwarfs: Ugly, Nerdy, Dumpy, and Cranky Pants."

"Which one am I?" Mandy piped up. "I wanna be Cranky Pants—that sounds like the best one."

Liberty rolled her eyes. "If you're talking about the best, then clearly you mean our team—not yours."

Scarlett stepped between them. "Guys, please! Cool it! Toni said no talking to the competition."

"Yeah! I'm not allowed to tell you our secrets," Gracie said, pointing a finger in Mandy's face.

"What secrets?" Mandy asked. "I bet our secrets are better than yours!"

Phoebe put a hand over Mandy's mouth, and Scarlett clamped her hand over Gracie's. "Zip the lip!" she warned her little sister. "Do you want Toni to kill us?"

Gracie shook her head. "Uh-uh." She turned to face the Feet. "I'm not telling you anything about my joker costume. So there!"

"Joker costume? Are you doing some lame Batman dance?" Addison asked. "Who's the Penguin? Your big sis, Scoot?"

"Hah! You're not even close!" Gracie said, just as Scarlett and Rochelle dragged her away.

"Gracie, you almost gave it away!" Anya exclaimed. "This is why we can't let you anywhere near our competition."

Scarlett sighed. "Like I said. Loose lips."

"Well, maybe they'll think we're doing a superheroes dance," Bria suggested. "With comic book villains."

"Maybe we should let them think that," Rochelle said, raising a brow. "I mean, if they want to believe it, we can't stop them, right?"

Liberty's eyes lit up. "You mean feed them false info?" she asked. "I'm liking this already! Can't you just see Justine switching their routine last minute to try and ruin ours?"

Anya considered. "I don't think it's right to lie, but Gracie did kind of tip our hand."

"Exactly!" Liberty said. "We're just covering our tracks. Toni would totally approve of a little white lie to protect ourselves."

"I don't know about that," Scarlett hesitated. "But I guess we don't have much of a choice, do we?"

Liberty took Gracie by the shoulders. "Okay, we need you to blab a little secret to Mandy."

Gracie looked confused. "But my lips are zipped, remember?"

"Unzip 'em!" Liberty insisted. "This is what you tell her: you're the Joker, Scarlett's the Penguin, and I'm Batgirl."

"How come you always get the biggest role?" Rochelle asked. "Tell her *I'm* Batgirl, Liberty is Robin, and Anya is the Penguin."

Bria raised her hand. "What am I? Chopped liver? I wanna be Batgirl!"

"It's not like this is for real!" Rochelle reminded her.

"Huh? I don't get it," Gracie said. "Why am I telling Mandy this?"

Liberty gave her a shove in the direction of City Feet. "Because we want them to think it's our group routine. Got it?"

Gracie nodded. "Got it." She went up to Mandy and tapped her on the shoulder.

"I have something to say to you," she began, then hesitated. It was hard to remember everything her teammates had told her! "Okay, Scarlett and Rochelle are penguins with baseball bats and Anya and Bria are chopped liver—oh, and I'm joking. Or something like that . . ."

Mandy looked confused. "I don't get the joke. Is it a knock-knock?"

Gracie smiled. "Oh! I know a great joke! How do you make a tissue dance?"

Mandy thought for a few seconds. "I don't know. How?"

"You put a little boogie in it! Ha-ha!" Gracie was cracking up—and planning on telling another joke—just as Liberty stepped in to break up the conversation.

"Okay, Gracie. Time to go! Hope you didn't let the cat out of the bag."

"Cat? You said it was a bat!" Gracie complained. "Would you people make up your minds?"

Liberty ushered the little girl back to the Divas. "Mission accomplished," she said, patting Gracie on the back. "They were chattering away, so I'm sure Mandy will go running back to Justine with all the info."

As the Divas had predicted, Mandy couldn't wait to report the news to her teammates. "I know what dance the Divas are doing," she said, tugging on Phoebe's sleeve. "They're doing a baseball number with chopped liver."

"What?" Phoebe asked. "That doesn't make any sense."

"No, it's true!"

"Are you sure?" Addison asked her. "Maybe you got it a little mixed up. Like in that game telephone when the message gets all garbled?"

Mandy stamped her foot. "I know what Gracie said! She said they have bats and the song is called 'Penguin Boogie.'"

"It sounds bizarre," Regan weighed in. "Are you sure Gracie wasn't pulling your leg?"

Mandy stared down at her sweatpants. "She didn't pull my leg. She just tapped me on the shoulder."

"Then again, it *could* be really creative," Addison pointed out. "I wouldn't put it past Toni and her Dance Duds. Our group dance *is* kinda predictable. We better tell Justine."

CHAPTER 13

Family Crisis

In the middle of Anya and Rochelle's duet rehearsal, Mrs. Bazarov burst into the room.

"I'm sorry to interrupt, but it's an emergency," she said. Anya could tell from her eyes that she'd been crying.

"What is it, Mom?" she asked, running to her. "Is everything okay?"

"No. It's your brother. He was in a car accident and he's in the hospital."

"Is it bad, Felice?" Toni asked gently.

"He has a concussion, some broken ribs," she replied. "My husband says they're doing scans right now to make sure there's no internal bleeding. He was so excited to get his license . . ."

Anya felt like everything was happening in slow motion. What if Alexei needed surgery—or worse? "We have to go home to him, right now!" she cried. "Please, Mom!"

Rochelle gasped. "But Anya! The competition!"

Anya turned to Toni. "I don't know what to do," she said, tears streaming down her cheeks. "I don't want to let you or the Divas down, but my brother needs me."

Toni hugged her. "Of course he does. And you're not letting us down. We'll make it work."

"Really? You're not mad?" Anya asked her coach.

"I'd be mad if you didn't show loyalty to your family," Toni replied. "Isn't that what I always teach you girls? Loyalty first?"

Anya nodded and raced out of the studio with her mom to catch a flight back to L.A.

Rochelle sat in the middle of the rehearsal room floor, stunned.

"You thought I was going to make Anya stay and see the competition through, didn't you?" Toni asked her.

Rochelle shrugged. "It was just really nice of you to let Anya go. That's all I'm saying."

"Good. Because you're going to do this entire magic duet as a solo now."

Rochelle gasped. "It doesn't work as a solo; it's meant for two people!"

"It will be meant for one person when I get through with it," Toni said, her voice trailing off in thought. "I wonder where I can rent a couple of doves for a few hours . . ."

Four hours later, Rochelle reappeared in the room where the rest of the girls had been trying on their card costumes and warming up.

"You look like you've been through a war," Bria said, noticing Rock's tangled hair and wrinkled shirt. "Ew! What's that gooey white stuff on your shoulder?"

"Dove poop," Rochelle said, collapsing on the floor. "But it's not as bad as when they nip you with their beaks. That really hurts!"

"I don't wanna know," Scarlett said, and sighed.

"This sounds like a last-minute Toni extreme dance makeover," Bria said. "If you look this bad, I can't imagine what Anya must look like."

"Anya's gone," Rochelle said.

"Gone?" Gracie asked. "Where did she go? To the bathroom?"

"Probably to shower off the dove poop," Liberty said, smirking.

"No. She's gone home to L.A. for good," Rochelle replied. "She was planning on telling you guys after the competition, but her brother was in a bad car accident today. She and her mom flew home to be with him at the hospital."

"That's awful! But I don't get it," Bria replied. "You said for good. You mean Anya isn't coming back to Divas? *Ever?*"

Rochelle shook her head. "Her parents decided they wanted the family to be together in L.A. That's the secret she was keeping till after this weekend. This was going to be her last competition."

Scarlett shook her head. "I can't imagine Divas without her. What will we do?" She looked at Liberty who—for the very first time—was speechless.

"What?" Liberty asked her teammate. "What do you want me to say? I'm not happy about it either. Anya was the best ballet dancer we've ever had."

"She was the best friend we've ever had," Bria said. "I can't believe this is happening!"

Just then, Toni barged in. "I take it that Rochelle has shared the news with you about Anya's quick departure," she said. "So we have our work cut out for us."

Liberty suddenly stood up, furious. "That's it? We have our work cut out for us? One of our Divas is gone and that's all you can say?"

Toni's cheeks flushed. "I know you're upset that we have to redo the group dance, but I will not tolerate that tone of voice from you, Liberty."

"But Anya's never coming back!" Gracie piped up. "I miss her already!"

Toni looked shocked. "You're telling me that Anya is leaving Divas?"

"She told Rock," Scarlett explained. "She was going to tell us all after Smooth Moves. It's not her fault. Her parents won't let her live in New Jersey anymore."

"I see," Toni said simply. "Well, we'll deal with that once the competition is over. Anya wanted it that way, and we owe it to her to win." She turned to Liberty. "Don't you agree?"

Liberty stared down at her feet. "Fine."

"Okay, then," Toni said, clapping her hands together. "Time to reshuffle this 'House of Cards' dance."

CHAPTER 14

Making Magic

The next morning, bright and early, the Divas, their moms, and Miss Toni all reported to the Las Vegas Convention Center. "Game faces on," Toni insisted as they walked backstage to their dressing room. "I know we're all sad about Anya, but that is not going to get in the way of our dancing today. Do I make myself clear?" The girls all nodded sadly.

Toni checked the program. "Preteen solos at 10:00 a.m. Scarlett. Get changed and run your routine."

"Have you heard from Anya at all?" Scarlett whispered to Rochelle.

Rochelle looked worried. "I tried texting and calling but she doesn't answer. I hope everything's okay."

Scarlett climbed into her costume: a white chiffon dress spotted with black dots. "You look like 101 Dalmatians," Gracie told her sister. "Are you supposed to be a puppy, Scoot?"

"I'm supposed to be rolling the dice," she said, demonstrating a graceful turn.

"Make sure you extend those arms," Toni instructed her. "And keep the movements flowing. No breaks between."

Finally, the announcer summoned her to the stage: "Performing a modern routine, here is Scarlett dancing 'Superstition.'"

As she took her place on the stage, lying on her back and staring up at the ceiling, waiting for her music to begin, Scarlett couldn't help thinking about Anya. She saw her sitting in a cold hospital waiting room, ringing her hands and worrying about Alexei. Scarlett knew how worried she'd be if Gracie was ever hurt. Her mind wandered off, and before she realized it, she had missed her opening cue.

She quickly rolled on her stomach and stretched her hands out to the audience. Maybe the judges wouldn't notice she was a few beats behind. The music was slightly haunting, with whispers of wind and hints of chimes in the distance. She got on her knees and stretched backward, twisting from side to side in one graceful, fluid motion. She poured her heart and soul into the dance, letting all the sadness about Anya leaving pour out of her.

"Whoa, she's killin' it!" Rochelle said, watching from the wings.

For her last move, Miss Toni had told her to "be a wave crashing across the sand." So she rolled across the stage, letting the layers of her skirt fall around her like the foamy water. The judges were mesmerized. Finally, she kneeled, hugged her arms around her shoulders, and bowed her head as the lights dimmed to black. It was a good thing the audience couldn't see her face—there were tears streaming down her cheeks and her bottom lip was quivering.

"Good job," Toni said as Scarlett raced backstage and dabbed her eyes with a layer of her skirt. "You were in the moment, and it showed."

Scarlett nodded. "I just can't stop thinking about Anya," she said. "I feel like there's a big hole in my heart."

"I know," Toni whispered to her. "We all feel that way. And you did the right thing. You found a way to channel the emotion into your dance."

Next up was Rochelle with her rechoreographed routine without Anya. Toni handed her a top hat. "Keep it together," she warned her. "Smooth and controlled."

Rochelle checked her pockets and her jacket sleeves to make sure all her props were in place. "I'll do my part," she assured Toni. "But I make no promises for your little feathered friends."

"Performing a Broadway-style routine to *Pippin*'s 'Magic to Do,' please put your hands together for Rochelle!" the announcer said.

"Here goes nothing," Rochelle whispered into her collar. "Doves, do your best!"

She shimmied across the stage dressed as Leading Player in a top hat, black leotard, and tuxedo jacket with tails. As the voices on the track crooned, "Ooh, ooh, oooh," she wiggled her hips and twirled a magic wand in her hand. With a wave, it suddenly sprouted a bouquet of flowers. The audience applauded as she tossed it to the front row. Next, she did a series of *fouetté* turns and the doves flew out of her hidden jacket pockets. Another dove popped out of her hat as she took it off and tipped it at the judges.

"OMG! That is sick!" Bria cheered from the wings. "Go, Rock!"

Suddenly, she reached above her head and grabbed a trapeze that appeared from the ceiling. She flipped upside down and twirled high above the stage, hanging upside down by her knees.

As the trapeze lowered, she descended into a split and ended her routine by waving her wand at the judges. In the blink of an eye, the wand vanished in thin air. The audience jumped to their feet and applauded wildly.

"That was amazing!" Scarlett said, hugging her friend as she came off the stage. "I'm calling you the Wizard of Rock from now on!"

Phoebe was waiting for her turn and overheard them. "Don't you mean the Wizard of Pathetic?" she asked, smirking. "I have a Broadway dance solo, too. And it's gonna blow yours away—literally." She strutted out onstage as the announcer read, "Please welcome Phoebe, performing 'Let's Go Fly a Kite' from *Mary Poppins* . . ."

Rochelle stuck her head out from behind the curtain to watch. Phoebe's costume was an intricate dress made of individual handkerchiefs in shades of blue, white, and silver. She twirled and swirled around the stage, holding a kite magically suspended by an invisible wire.

"She's *gooood*," Bria said. "Really good."

"Please, don't rub it in!" Rochelle said, covering her eyes with her hand. "If she flies up in the air like a kite, I'm gonna lose it."

Phoebe did a graceful *arabesque*, then—just as Rochelle had feared—flew up, up, up to the ceiling where she performed an aerial ballet thirty feet above the ground. The judges craned their heads to watch.

"It's Vegas. Justine is pulling out all the stops," Toni said with a sigh. "Hopefully the judges will see past all the smoke and mirrors and appreciate our technique."

"Or not," Liberty said, motioning to the panel, who was applauding every move enthusiastically. "We're doomed."

"Not yet we're not," said a voice behind them.

"Anya!" Gracie squealed, running to hug her teammate around the waist. "You're back!"

All the girls gathered around her.

"How's your bro?" Rochelle asked. "Is he okay?"

"Alex is fine, thank goodness," Anya replied. "Just some bumps and bruises and two broken ribs. But he'll be good as new."

"Which is why I let Anya come back," Mrs. Bazarov said. "We caught an early flight this morning from L.A. She didn't want to leave her Diva family when they needed her."

"I brought my costume," she told Toni. "Can I still be in the group dance?"

Toni tapped her finger to her lips. "I'm not sure . . ."

"What? Are you nuts? City Feet is creaming us!" Liberty shouted.

"What she means is we have a much stronger routine with Anya in it," Scarlett said, putting her arm around Anya. "Wasn't that what you were trying to tell Miss Toni, Liberty?"

"Fine, what she said," Liberty said grumpily.

"I wish you had been honest with me, Anya," Toni said firmly. "I don't like surprises."

"I wasn't trying to surprise anyone," Anya insisted. "I just didn't know how to tell you all that I was moving back to L.A."

"Honesty is always the best policy," Toni replied. "But there's no sense in discussing that now. Get into your costume. We have thirty minutes before Junior Group dance is up."

"Hooray!" Gracie cheered. "Anya's back!"

The Divas were up fourth, right after Razzmatazz, Pink Ladies Rock, and City Feet.

"I don't get it—what's with the leopard-skin togas and the clubs?" Bria asked, watching the Razzmatazz boys race past her onto the stage. The tallest one was pounding his chest and yelling, "Yabba dabba doo!"

"They're doing a routine to *The Flintstones* theme," Rochelle explained. "Though why, I have no idea." The choreography was certainly primitive, with each of the boys walking on their hands and hopping around the stage barefoot. The last part of the routine consisted of them hoisting a giant rock over their heads.

"That was certainly interesting," Bria commented.

"Remember what Miss Toni always says," Anya reminded them. "The judges always give high points to boy dance teams."

Next up was Pink Ladies Rock performing an acro routine dressed in pajamas to Katy Perry's "Waking Up in Vegas."

"Yawn," Liberty quipped. "This number's putting me to sleep."

"That was a pretty impressive back handspring," Bria noted. Just then, all six girls ripped off their pj's onstage to reveal Vegas showgirl costumes in vibrant shades of red, orange, and gold. They *pirouetted* around the stage effortlessly, and the lead dancer did an impressive twenty *fouettés* in a row.

"Whoa! That was amazing!" Anya commented. "I thought we had just City Feet to worry about today, but all the teams are bringing it."

When it was time for City Feet's group number, only Mandy was waiting in the wings.

"Where's the rest of your team?" Rochelle asked her. "Did the rest of Stinky Feet chicken out?"

Mandy kept her mouth shut and ignored her taunting. She was wearing a silver leotard and a long platinum wig.

"Performing a contemporary acro routine to Lady Gaga's 'Poker Face,' please welcome City Feet!" the announcer boomed over the microphone.

"Gaga? Did he say Gaga?" Liberty whined. "I told you people we should have used her costume designer!"

Mandy tumbled out onstage as the rest of her teammates appeared in a cloud of smoke. They each wore a crazy costume inspired by Lady Gaga: Phoebe was in a green unitard with a boa made from furry stuffed frogs; Addison wore a red lace bodysuit and a crown covering her face; Regan was in a black-and-white triangular mask and a white leotard covered in plastic bubbles.

"What's next? A flying saucer landing in the middle of the convention center, carrying Elvis?" Rochelle groaned.

"Awesome! Where?" Gracie asked.

"Guys! Am I seeing this?" Scarlett directed their attention back to the stage. "Is Phoebe carrying a baseball bat?"

"They all are!" Bria chimed in. "They must have believed what Mandy told them."

Each of the Feet paraded around the stage, swinging baseball bats in the air. Addison and

Regan even tossed a ball between them while Mandy did a cartwheel around third base.

"But we said Batgirl, not baseball bat!" Anya said. "Where did they get that idea?"

"I dunno, but it's a hoot!" Rochelle burst out laughing. "Lady Gaga sliding into home plate. It's so wrong!"

"You can say that again," Toni said, finding her team in a fit of hysterical laughter. "It's a very disjointed routine. I understand the Gaga-esque costumes, but what's with the baseball diamond? Do you have any idea *what* Justine might be trying to say?"

"She's saying, 'Someone gave me some wrong 411!'" Rochelle roared. "OMG, this is a riot!"

Gracie raised her hand. "I let the bat out of the bag."

"You did what?" Toni replied. "Who put you up to this?"

"We didn't *tell* them to do it," Liberty said, defending the Divas' actions. "We just sort of whispered in Mandy's ear."

"And what's in her ear is outta her mouth," Rochelle added. "But I guess something got lost in translation. When Gracie accidentally told all the Feet she was wearing a Joker costume, we had to cover our tracks. So we kinda told her to tell Mandy we were doing a Batman-themed routine."

"Bat as in creepy black-winged thing that turns into a vampire," Liberty pointed out to her youngest teammate. "Not let's play ball!"

"I see," Toni replied. "So you lied to them and they took the bait?"

"Exactly!" Liberty exclaimed. "It's not our fault at all."

Anya braced herself. She could feel a long lecture coming on from their dance coach. "We were just trying to save our number," she said.

Toni clasped her hands behind her back. "Did I not tell all of you to stay away from the competition and not speak a word to them?"

"Liberty talked first," Gracie said. "Then Rock, then me."

"I'm sure they did," their teacher said. "But you're all just as guilty. I have to go find Justine now and apologize to her—which is something I *hate* doing."

"Could it maybe wait till *after* we beat them?" Scarlett asked. "Like a 'no hard feelings' kind of thing?"

"Cheaters never win," Toni answered. "But I suppose Justine cheated in changing her routine to copy ours."

"We all know Justine's batty anyway," Liberty quipped. "I say we forget it ever happened."

"I say you go out there and win us first place," Toni insisted. "Then I'll decide how to handle your fibbing to the Feet."

CHAPTER 15

House of Cards

As City Feet strutted off the stage, Liberty raised her hand to high-five them.

"Nice," she said. "What do you call that routine—'Four Strikes You're Out'?"

"I call it a winner," Regan replied. "Especially when you go out there and do your pathetic best to copy it."

"Oh, you mean the baseball thing?" Rochelle asked. "Yeah, it's not happening."

Mandy's mouth hung open. "Huh? Gracie said you were doing a dance with baseball bats!"

"You shouldn't believe everything you hear," Bria pointed out.

"I told you we should have put in chopped liver and penguins," Gracie said, pouting. "You guys need to trust me more!"

Liberty pushed Regan aside. "Out of the way," she said. "Let us show you how it's done."

The Divas took their places on the three-tiered platform Toni had built. They waited patiently for the host to announce them: "Performing a jazz number to 'Luck Be a Lady,' please welcome, Dance Divas in 'House of Cards'!"

As they had rehearsed, Rochelle ducked down to let Gracie leapfrog high over her head. Gracie's shoes and hat were trimmed in jingly bells that tinkled as she flipped and flitted around the stage. Each girl brought her own character and style to her role: Anya's ace was a delicate ballerina *en pointe*; Rochelle's jack was a cool and confident hip-hop dancer break dancing on the floor; Bria's ten of diamonds did a sparkling tap time step; and Liberty and Scarlett were a lyrical king and queen in all their royal splendor. Liberty's crown twinkled under the stage lights as she pranced around in a white vinyl catsuit with green and purple piping. They did an impressive fifteen *fouetté* turns in perfect sync before Liberty hit a switch on her waistband to reveal a "hidden" element of her costume: all the seams lit up and flashed in time to the music!

The audience oohed and aahed, especially when Gracie stood on Rock's shoulders and jumped onto a trampoline. When she bounced back up in the air, she did a forward somersault. At the end of the number, all the girls stood in a line and fell backward, like a house of cards toppling over. There was thunderous applause and whistling; one judge gave them two enthusiastic thumbs-up.

As they dashed off the stage, Toni grabbed Liberty by the elbow. "What happened to doing your costume without any help?" she asked. "How many electricians did it take to rig up those flashing lights?"

"None," Liberty insisted. "It was actually an old Halloween costume that I found at my next-door neighbor's yard sale." She showed Toni the label on the back: it read BUZZ LIGHTYEAR.

"So you recycled it?" Toni asked her.

"Yup, and I glued all the gems on the crown myself," she said, taking off her headpiece. "Scout's honor!"

"You're not a Girl Scout," Rochelle pointed out.

"Okay, then Diva's honor. I really did it all myself. My mom was way too busy choreographing Pitbull, and I needed something to do in the hotel all day."

Toni nodded. "Then you did a great job, which I hope teaches you a lesson—you don't need to rely on your mom's help or connections."

Liberty smiled. It felt good to do something by herself for once. "Who knew?"

"I did," Toni replied with a wink.

Now, all that was left was to await the judges' decisions. Anya crossed her fingers and hoped that their "House of Cards" routine was enough to beat everyone else's over-the-top productions. Except for Liberty's light show, their number didn't have lots of bells and whistles—unless you counted the bells on Gracie's costume!

The announcer summoned everyone's attention as the teams sat onstage, hoping to hear their names. City Feet took home first prize for best duet (Phoebe and Addison's slot-machine tap routine "Ring Them Bells"), and Mandy won Mini Solo (for her acro routine to "Going to the Chapel").

"They're gonna sweep." Anya sighed. "I can't stand it!"

"We don't know that yet," Scarlett tried to comfort her. "Preteen Solo is up next. Fingers crossed."

"My toes are crossed," Rochelle replied. "In case that helps."

"In third place, Dance Divas, 'Magic to Do'!" The host read the judges' ruling.

Rochelle accepted her plaque and returned to her seat. "Oh well," she said. "I can't win 'em all."

She squeezed Scarlett's hand. "I hope you take it home for Divas."

"In second place," the announcer continued. "Also from Dance Divas, 'Superstition'!"

Scarlett collected her plaque and looked equally disappointed. Anya couldn't help but think that this was all her fault. She'd distracted and upset all her teammates—and now they were paying the price. She caught a glimpse of Miss Toni in the audience. Steam was coming out of her ears.

"You know who that leaves in first place . . . ," Scarlett whispered.

The announcer finished her sentence: "'Let's Go Fly a Kite,' City Feet!"

Phoebe skipped up to receive her trophy. She held it above her head and blew kisses to the audience. Justine stood on her seat and cheered with the rest of the City Feet moms.

Anya felt sick to her stomach.

"There's still Junior Group dance," Bria reminded her.

"We might as well just hand the trophy to Justine," Liberty said. "So she can start gloating now."

This time, when the announcer got to second place, there were three teams remaining: Razzmatazz, City Feet, and Dance Divas.

"What if we don't even place?" Anya asked, biting her nails. "I can't take the suspense!"

The announcer studied the card. "In second place, 'Caveman Shuffle,' Razzmatazz!"

Anya held her breath. "That means it's them . . . or us."

The Divas waited for what felt like an eternity for the announcer to read the first-place team name. "Congratulations, City Feet!" he exclaimed, as Phoebe, Addison, Regan, and Mandy jumped up and down.

"I don't believe it," Liberty moaned. "I told you we should have gone with Gaga."

"It wasn't the costumes," Scarlett insisted. "I guess the judges thought their dance was really creative—bats and all."

"Yeah, thanks to us for giving them the idea," Rochelle complained.

"Just a second! May I have your attention please!" the announcer broke in over the celebration. "We have a tie for first place. Congratulations also to 'House of Cards,' Dance Divas!"

Anya gasped. "Did he just say we won?" She grabbed Rochelle and shook her. "He said we won!"

They raced up to accept the trophy—right next to the girls of City Feet.

"Nice try sabotaging our number," Phoebe told Liberty. "Too bad you couldn't stop us from getting a clean sweep."

"Well, someone should sweep you out of here," Liberty replied. "That's what they do with garbage, isn't it?"

Toni was about to referee—and remind her girls to behave in public—when Justine stepped in.

"I don't think either of our teams deserves this," she announced to the judges. "And I think Toni would agree with me."

Toni nodded. "Absolutely. Both the Divas and City Feet behaved in an unsportsmanlike way," she said. "Justine and I feel first prize should go to Razzmatazz."

Anya couldn't believe what she was hearing! Was Toni actually forfeiting a first-place win? And even crazier, was she *agreeing* with Justine?

"I hope this teaches you all a lesson," Toni scolded her team. "What you did was wrong, and you don't deserve to hold your heads up as first-place winners." The boys from Razzmatazz grabbed the trophy out of Liberty's hand.

"Hey, Cave Boy!" Liberty threatened him. "Back off!"

"No, Justine and Toni are right," Scarlett said. "It was mean to trick City Feet."

"But they changed their dance to destroy ours!" Liberty protested.

"Which is why we are forfeiting as well," Justine replied. "In hindsight, it was wrong to use the information the girls gave me against you." She patted Toni on the back. "Besides, our team won the rest of our divisions anyway—and you lost. That's good enough for me!"

Toni gathered her team around her. "I know we're all disappointed, so I'm not going to rub it in," she began.

"Oh, thank goodness!" Rochelle heaved a sigh of relief. "I thought we were in for a lecture."

"Oh, you are," Toni replied. "But I thought I'd save it for the studio when we get home. You can think about it all the way home on the plane tomorrow."

Anya suddenly remembered she wasn't going back to New Jersey with her friends. "I wish I could have left on a high note," she said, hugging each of them. "But you'll win the next competition for me, right?"

Rochelle hugged her tight. "You bet. Those Feet better run!"

"We'll miss you so much," Scarlett said, welling up. "It just won't be the same without you."

"L.A. is so far away," Gracie sniffled. "Will you FaceTime me every day on Bria's computer?"

"You better!" Bria said, getting in on the group hug.

The only one who hadn't said good-bye was Liberty.

"You know my mom goes to Hollywood all the time," she told Anya. "I could go with her and visit you—if you want."

"That would be great," Anya said, holding her arms out for a hug.

Liberty wrinkled her nose. "I hate getting emotional. It makes my mascara run," she sniffed.

Anya smiled. "Okay, then let's just say, 'See you soon.'"

Finally, it was Toni's turn. "Anya, I saw something very special in you from the very first time we met," she said. "And I'm never wrong."

Anya nodded. "Thanks for letting me join your team, Miss Toni. I'll never forget any of you or any of our crazy adventures."

"Maybe you don't have to," Mrs. Bazarov interrupted. "Alexei has something to tell you." She handed her cell phone to Anya.

"Dude," said a weak voice on the other end.

"Alex, are you okay?" she asked.

"I'm more than okay," he answered. "I got into NYU film school, starting next year. The admissions letter came yesterday, when I was in the hospital, so I never got to open it. I'm in!"

"What? That's amazing!" Anya said. "You're gonna be a famous director!"

"And since both of our kids seemed determined to be on the East Coast, your dad and I decided we give up," her mom added. "We'll just have to move to New Jersey over the summer and set up Frosty on the lawn there."

"You mean it?" Anya said. "I don't have to leave Divas?"

"If they want you, they can keep you," her mom replied, and smiled.

"We want her! We want her!" her teammates cheered.

Anya looked at Miss Toni. "Is it okay if I stay?"

"Oh, I suppose," Toni said with a wink. "I think I have a spot open."

CHAPTER 16

Read My Lips

When they got back to New Jersey, Toni had a brilliant idea how to teach her team a thing or two about keeping their mouths shut.

"So, I call this group dance 'Our Lips Are Sealed,'" she said, hitting the button on her iPod. A bubbly '80s pop song by the Go-Go's filled the studio and the girls began to bop around to it. She handed Gracie a roll of pink duct tape.

"This will be part of your costume," she instructed her. "Each of you will have your own color, and I'd like it wrapped around your leotards creatively. Oh, and also across your lips."

She broke off a small piece and put it on Gracie's mouth. Gracie giggled.

"Are you kidding me? That is so unglam!" Liberty complained.

"Really? I thought you would say that," Toni replied. She handed Liberty a photo of Lady Gaga wearing an outfit made of yellow police tape. "That's why I took the idea from Gaga herself."

"Oh," Liberty said softly. "Whatever."

"I want to make it perfectly clear that we don't keep secrets from each other or tell false ones to the competition."

"Even if it's a really good one?" Gracie asked.

"Especially if it's a really good one," their teacher replied.

When each of the girls had secured a piece of tape over her mouth, Miss Toni read off the list of upcoming competitions. "We'll be ending March in Michigan; then on to Philly, Delaware, Erie, and finally Los Angeles for Nationals—if we qualify."

Anya raised her hand. "Yes, Anya, you can talk."

Anya peeled the tape off her lips. "Do you think my brother, Alexei, can come to Nationals and shoot us rehearsing? He wants to make a dance documentary for film school in the fall."

Toni nodded. "I don't see why not."

Liberty's hand went up as well.

"I know I'll regret this, but yes, Liberty, you can speak, too," Toni said.

"I think I should star in the documentary," Liberty suggested. "I mean, I am the most talented and glamorous Diva, right?" She turned to Rochelle who was still wearing the tape on her mouth. "Anything to say about that, Rock?"

Instead of protesting, Rochelle took a piece of tape and secured it back across Liberty's lips.

"Thank you," Miss Toni said, rubbing her temples. "We've got a long way to go before Nationals, and I'm not making any decisions till right before."

She ran the girls through the jazz routine several times, then had them gather around her in a circle when they were done.

"I've decided to hold rehearsals during part of spring break," she informed her team. The Divas groaned in unison—it meant cutting their vacation short.

"Seriously? My family was planning a trip to my Pappy Hee-Haw's in Alabama," Rochelle complained.

"I knew it. I knew if we got a week off in February, we'd pay for it later on," Liberty muttered.

"There goes the trip to Canada with Dad, Gracie," Scarlett said. "I was so psyched to see our cousins in Montreal."

The only one not upset was Anya. "My dad and bro are coming out here for a week," she said. "And I really can't think of anywhere else I want to be than here with all of you."

Rochelle hugged her. "That goes double for all of us."

Toni smiled. As much as her girls kept her on her toes, they also reminded her why she loved her job so much. They might bicker, but they truly cared about each other. She faced them all and clapped her hands above her head to get their attention: "Now you're talking!"

Glossary of Dance Terms

Arabesque: a move where the dancer stands on one leg with the other leg extended behind her at 90 degrees.

Barre: the wooden bar in the ballet studio that a dancer holds on to with one or both hands to practice/balance.

Cambre back: a bend from the waist to the back.

Chaîné: a series of quick turns.

En pointe: literally on the point of your toes; dancing in pointe shoes.

Fouetté: a turning step where the leg whips out to the side.

Frappé: when a dancer beats her toe against her supporting foot's ankle.

Tendu: the leg slides out to the front, back, or side, remaining straight all the way to the point of the toe.

Sheryl Berk is a proud ballet mom and a *New York Times* bestselling author. She has collaborated with numerous celebrities on their memoirs, including Britney Spears, *Glee*'s Jenna Ushkowitz, and *Shake It Up*'s Zendaya. Her book with Bethany Hamilton, *Soul Surfer*, hit #1 on the *New York Times* bestseller list and became a major motion picture. She is also the author of The Cupcake Club book series with her daughter, Carrie.